Read-Along Songs

Especially for your classroom,
wishing you many hours of reading and singing fun!

Read-Along Songs is a project of
Family Reading Partnership
made possible with funding support from

IPEI
Ithaca Public Education Initiative

"To my mother, Marion Lyman Carlisle,

who has always sung to her children."

Book design by Lucy Nielsen and Vandy Ritter.
Typeset in CG Bernhard Modern and Papyrus. Printed in Hong Kong.
The illustrations in this book were rendered in pen and ink with watercolor.

Library of Congress Cataloging-in-Publication Data
Long, Sylvia.
Hush little baby / by Sylvia Long.
p. cm.
Summary: In this variation on an old lullaby, a baby rabbit is shown
an assortment of wonders by its adoring parent.
ISBN: 0-8118-1416-5
1. Folk songs, English—Texts.   II. Lullabies. 2. Folk songs.]
I. Title.
PZ8.3.L8555Hu   1997   96-28724
782.42162'21'00268—dc20   CIP
AC

Distributed in Canada by Raincoast Books
9050 Shaughnessy Street, Vancouver, British Columbia V6P 6E5

10 9

Chronicle Books LLC
85 Second Street, San Francisco, California 94105

www.chroniclebooks.com/Kids

Hush Little Baby

Sylvia Long

chronicle books · san francisco

A Note from Sylvia Long

As much as I love being an artist, my favorite and most important profession has been being a mother. I sang and read to my children, just as my mother sang and read to me. One of the songs that has bothered me as an adult is the original version of "Hush Little Baby." In it, a mama offers her baby comfort by promising to buy him or her all sorts of things (a mockingbird, a diamond ring, horse and cart, etc.). It seems much healthier to encourage children to find comfort in the natural things around them and the warmth of a mother's love. This belief was my inspiration for a new version, which I hope you will enjoy as much as I enjoyed creating it.

Sylvia Long

Hush little baby, don't say a word,

Mama's going to show you a hummingbird.

If that hummingbird should fly,
Mama's going to show you the evening sky.

When the nighttime shadows fall,
Mama's going to hear the crickets call.

While their song drifts from afar,

Mama's going to search for a shooting star.

When that star has dropped from view,
Mama's going to read a book with you.

When that story has been read,

Mama's going to bring your warm bedspread.

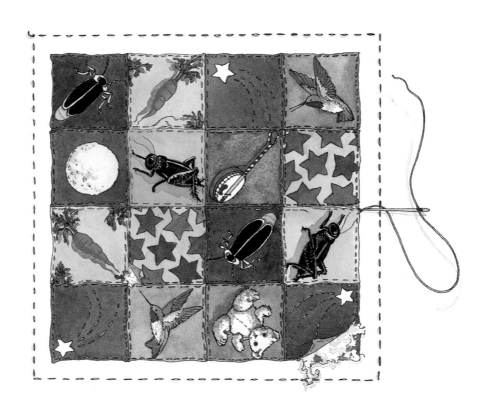

If that quilt begins to wear,

Mama's going to find your teddy bear.

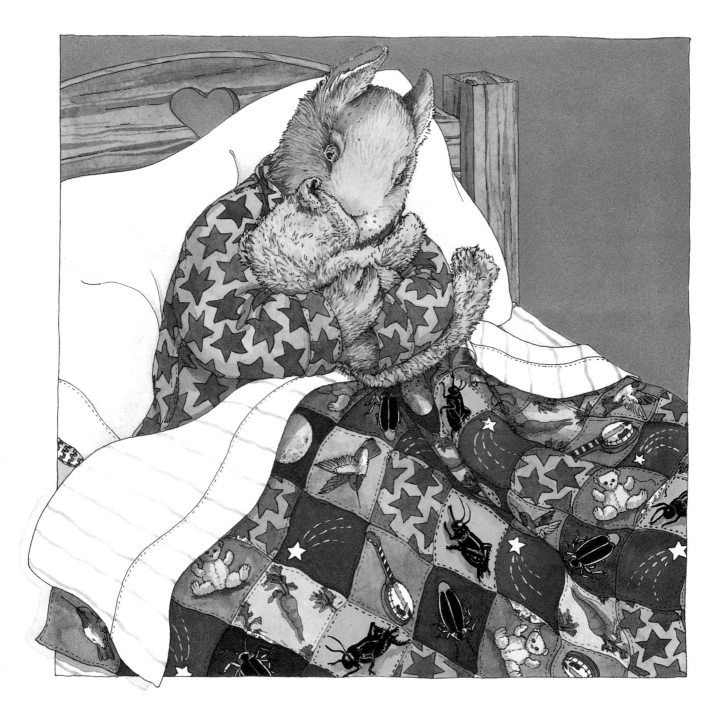

If that teddy bear won't hug,

Mama's going to catch you a lightning bug.

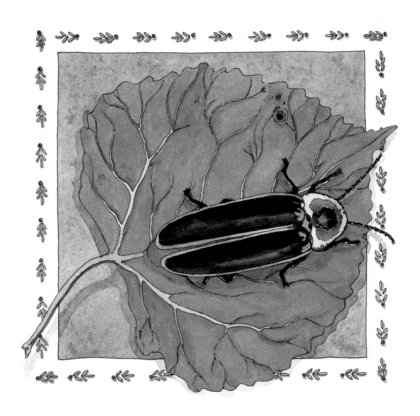

If that lightning bug won't glow,

Mama's going to play on her old banjo.

If that banjo's out of tune,

Mama's going to show you the harvest moon.

As that moon drifts through the sky,
Mama's going to sing you a lullaby.